This is **Tota**

You ~~can't~~ read
it **without**
having read
books 1,2,3,4
or 5.

WARNING
DO NOT EAT THIS BOOK!

You can also read this book without having eaten a <u>*grozint sandwich*</u>.

But if you get hungry halfway through, you'll have to *stop reading*, go make the sandwich and then **clear up**, and then eat it, which would *disturb your concentration...*

...*or*, you might find this story *so gripping* that you **can't put it down**, and then when you've finished you'll be so hungry **that you eat the actual book!**

Please DO NOT do it because:

[1] It's *not good* to eat books. **Really**.

[2] If you eat it, you won't be able to read it again.

[3] You also won't be able to **share it** with anyone.

Did you hear about the girl from the *north-west* corner of the *south-western* part of *west* **Western Swottolia**, who read Total Mayhem book 1* and loved it so much that she ate it *within 3 minutes* of reading the last page?

Into the Cave of Thieves

No, well I didn't
think so.

The poor thing.

She got rushed to
**The Hospital for
Totally Weird
Children** with a
terrible tummy ache.

And because of this
she missed her
final exams!

While she only had to spend one night in hospital and was fine, she had REALLY wanted to go to the **Nostril Vibrating Academy**, but was refused entry after missing the exams.

As a result, she had to go to **The Lawnmower Academy** where she trained as a lawnmower inspector.

Even though she came top of her class and had a great career, becoming Regional-Deputy-Chief-Inspector of her local area, a much-respected position, and lived a very happy life, we have to ask the question:

"What could have been?"

Perhaps she could have become **World Nostril Vibrating Champion?**

We will never know.

Anyway, don't worry about her.

She'll be fine.

It's actually quite nice being
a lawnmower inspector.

Now let's read
this book!

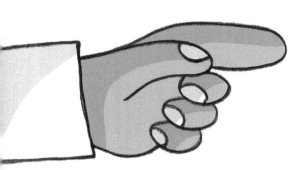

VBS (VERY BORING STUFF)

TOTAL MAYHEM 6
SATURDAY - DASH CANDOO AND THE MISSING DUCKS

CONTENTS

Created by Ralph Lazar.
Kneaded, massaged and
baked into shape by
Lisa Swerling.

CHARACTERS
SATURDAY

Dash Candoo and the Missing Ducks

Bridal couple
Names unknown

Henry the Hog
Warthog

Ms. Woodhouse
Art teacher

Dash Candoo
Hero of these stories

Rob Newman
Dash's best friend

Mr. Humma-Groff-Dwollop
Baker

Wombattina Triplets
Duck-feeders

Cynthia Blappy
Vertical
Tug-of-war
trainer

Zoo Lake Vertical Tug-of-war team

Mr. Darling
Math teacher

Rogina McRoger-Rogerson
Team captain and
Alpha-anchor

Oceanus Pomington
Captain of Industry

Feather-Scallywags
Enemy fighters

Mr. Clanwilliam
Owner of Zoo Lake
row boats

Chapter 1
A Day in Bed

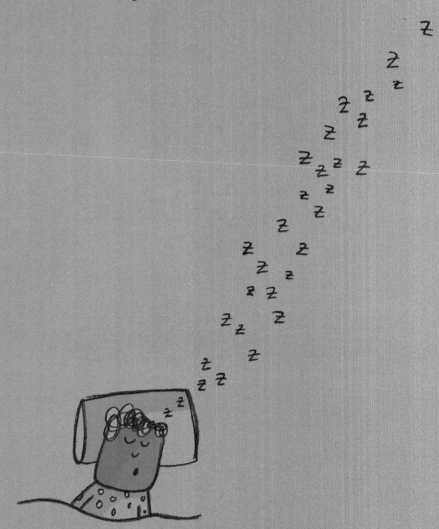

Aaah...
Saturday.

My *favorite* day of the week.

No school, so I get to

sleep late!

I *love* just lying in bed for hours **doing nothing** but *dozing* and **dreaming**.

Not really!

I set my <u>gralarm</u>
for 5am on
Saturdays.

Not a second of the weekend should be wasted!

Waaaaaaaaaaaaaay
too much to be done.

Ten tasks before heading
out:

Task [1]
Polish the family
rhinoceros.

And don't worry.
It's not a real rhinoceros.
It's a sculpture!

My *great*, **great**, great,
great, great, *great*,
great, great grandparents
came to this country by
boat with nothing but the
clothes on their backs, a
bag of carrots, and a
bronze statue of a
rhinoceros.

They **sold the carrots** and used the money to buy *carrot seeds*, and started a **carrot farm**, which eventually was a *success*.

Fortunately they were never desperate enough to be forced to sell the rhinoceros, and it has been in our family for generations now. My job is to polish it every weekend.

Task [2]
Feed Henry the Hog.

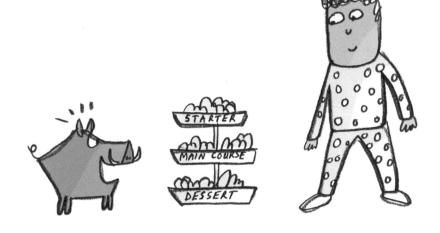

Henry is our pet warthog.

He smells.

It's a mix of *mildew*, **warthog** and duckpond.

I'm used to it by now.

And he's pretty cool.

Task [3]
Wake the ants.

By singing Kumbaya to them.

It's their *favourite* song.

Task [4]
Walk the ants.

I used to walk them *individually*, but these days there's too much to do, so I just walk them all in one go. Usually I do a *quick circuit* of our property, which takes approximately 15 minutes.

Kumbaya, my Lord, kumbaya
Kumbaya, my Lord, kumbaya
Kumbaya, my Lord, kumbaya
Oh, Lord, kumbaya

While walking them I am able to undertake tasks [5] and [6]:

Task [5]
Inspect Fortification & Escape Facilities.

This involves customary weekend inspection of my...

...bunker...

...treehouse...

...and escape tunnels.

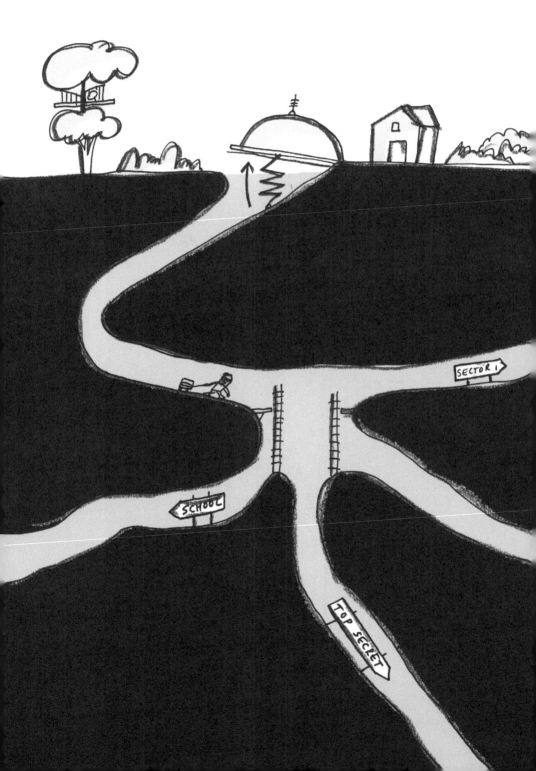

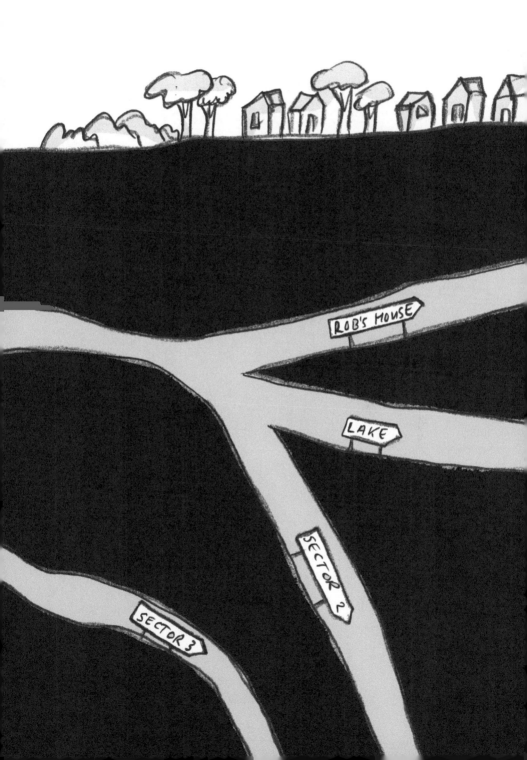

Task [6]
Inspect vegetable garden.

Everything looking good.
Especially *Sector C*
(carrots).

I LOVE carrots. Might it have
something to do with my great,
great, great, great, great,
great, great, great
grandparents?

Task [7]
Inspect surveillance tower.

This is on the top of our house *(above my bedroom)*. My house looks like a normal house, but my bedroom is **not** normal*.

My room

*It is highly *AB*normal, but I can't tell you about it right now. *It will have to wait till another time I'm afraid.*

Task [8]
Inspect my workshop.

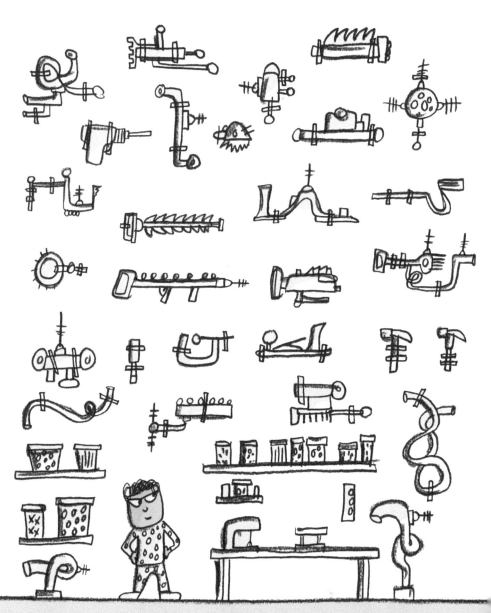

Task [9]
Tune my <u>quadcycle</u>.

And then,

Task [10]
Eat quick breakfast.

Today it was <u>reticulated</u> <u>basingstoke</u> and carrot juice.

It's important to start the day off with a good breakfast, **especially** on a Saturday!

Chapter 2
Zoo Lake

Okay, **breakfast done**.

I slung on my weekend
backpack, jumped onto my
quadcycle, and rode off
to Rob's house.

He's just a few houses
down.

I live at
#14 Glamorgan Rd.
He's at #22.

The moment I opened the gate, Henry the Hog *took the gap* **and was off**.

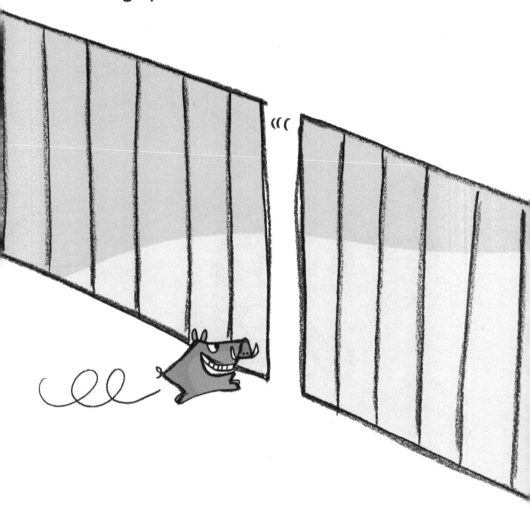

He also **loves** Saturdays, and like me, has **A LOT to do**.

Our plan was to **head down to Zoo Lake** (just two blocks away), circuit the lake, grab a snack at Mr. Humma-Groff-Dwollop, and then cruise through the outdoor art exhibition.

Our school art teacher, Ms. Woodhouse, was going to be exhibiting there.

Zoo Lake is often our adventure-ground on weekends.

The lake itself is exactly *one mile* in diameter, and is surrounded by a large park.

Here, look, this is a map
I made of it.

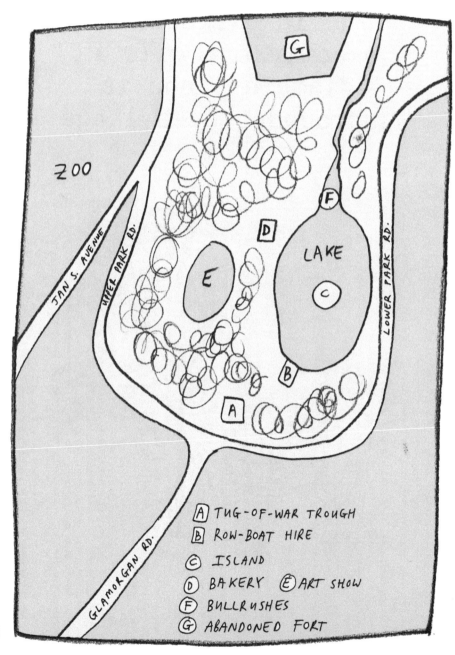

ZOO

JAN S. AVENUE

UPPER PARK RD.

LOWER PARK RD.

G

F

D

LAKE

E

C

B

A

GLAMORGAN RD.

Ⓐ TUG-OF-WAR TROUGH
Ⓑ ROW-BOAT HIRE
Ⓒ ISLAND
Ⓓ BAKERY Ⓔ ART SHOW
Ⓕ BULLRUSHES
Ⓖ ABANDONED FORT

Down to the lake we sped.

Zoo Lake is *covered* in ducks, the same flock that has been here for generations.

Everyone really LOVES them.

And they're not just *any old ducks*, they're <u>Fluff-tailed Hemple-fluffers</u>!

Visitors come from all **over the world** to admire them.

These ducks are **so rare** in fact, that the *only place they are found on earth* is right here, **at Zoo Lake!**

The Zoo Lake row boats
are **hugely** popular
because they let you get
really up-close to the
ducks.

And believe-you-me, getting *really-up close* to a Fluff-tailed Hemple-fluffer is an experience you'll **never** forget.

Rowing out to the ducks
is particularly popular
as a honeymoon* activity.

*The newlyweds tend to
stay at the VERY fancy
hotel, **The Duck Inn.**

Down at the lake, we rode
past the <u>Vertical
Tug-of-war</u> trough where
the Zoo Lake team
was in training for the
upcoming **World
Championships**.

They are coached by
Cynthia Blappy, the
world's most famous (*and
ferocious*) Vertical
Tug-of-war team trainer
(*obviously you've heard
of her*), which is why
they are expected to win
this year.

And just to *refresh your memory*, Vertical Tug-of-war is like **regular** Tug-of-war except it's vertical. The rope is thrown over a beam and the aim is to lift the other team off the ground.

It can be **really funny** to watch.

Up ahead we saw Henry run **under the legs** of Rogina McRoger-Rogerson, team captain and **Alpha-anchor** *(the person at the end of the rope).*

Rogina got such a
fright that she **let
go of the rope**.

They were
not happy
with Henry.

We *of course* pretended we
didn't know him.

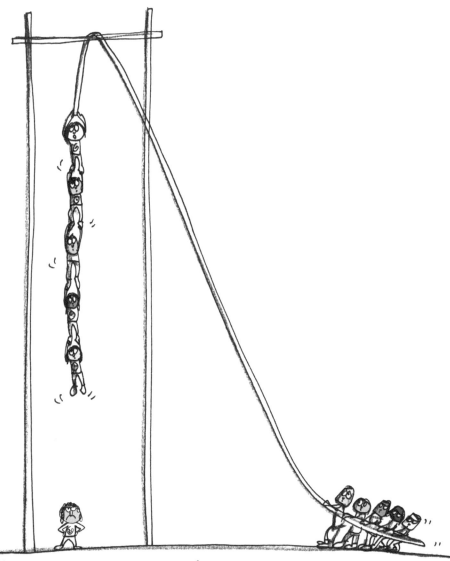

Then we spotted
Mr. Darling.

He'd just rented a boat
and was taking his
<u>pinkfish</u> out for
a little row.

We approached the
row-boat station.
Mr. Clanwilliam, the
owner, was just ushering
a bridal couple into a
boat...

...when Henry ran *between his legs.*

The groom and bride were
thrown out and then
**the whole boat
capsized.**

The resulting wave
knocked over
Mr. Darling's boat...

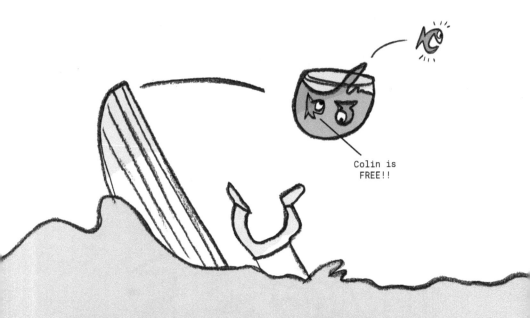

Colin is
FREE!!

...and his pinkfish
went floating off.

Lucky
fish!

Luckily he grabbed them in the nick of time.

Send us postcards!

The bride was **yelling at the groom** who was *yelling at Mr. Clanwilliam* who was **yelling at Henry**.

And Mr. Darling was yelling at them all.

Wow - whose warthog is that anyway?

Absolutely no idea!

Then we passed the
Wombattina Triplets*.

They are *amazing*.
Born 111 years ago,
they've been feeding the
ducks **every day** for the
last century. A large
gaggle of ducks had
gathered around them.

*Winnifred, Winona and Wilhemina.

This was **too much** for
Henry the Hog.

He ran straight
for them.

A Total Hog-vs-Duck Situation...

...and all three ladies
landed up in the water.

Wilhemina then started
screaming at Winona who
was screaming at
Winnifred who was
screaming at Henry.

The owner of that crazy warthog really is irresponsible, in my humble opinion.

We were getting hungry so
we sped up and headed to
Mr. Humma-Groff-Dwollop.

Time for a treat!

Chapter 3
Art and Snozzles

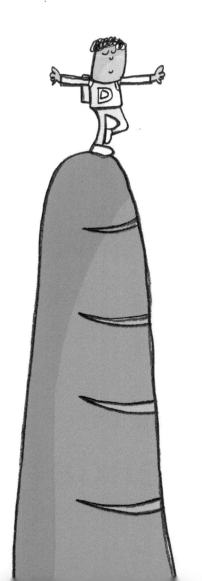

Mr. Humma-Groff-Dwollop
is one of the **world's
most famous bakers**.

His baguettes are
legendary.

They are **delicious**, and
of course, with their
inbuilt shoulder curl,
they're really **satisfying**
to carry.

A Mr. Humma-
Groff-Dwollop
baguette

Regular
baguette

Quite
satisfying
to carry

Unbelievably
satisfying
to carry

The ducks **love** the baguettes too.
Very useful to have a bakery in your backyard, especially if you're a duck.

No wonder the Fluff-tailed Hemple-fluffers **adore** Mr. Humma-Groff-Dwollop.

We bought one
baguette each, and
then cycled on.

Delicious!

The outdoor art exhibition
had already been set up.

We parked our quadcycles
up a tree and went to
enjoy the art.

This month the theme was

DUCKS!

Actually, I'm joking,
the theme is ALWAYS
ducks.

That's how much
everyone around here
loves the Zoo Lake
ducks.

While we were admiring a **particularly** amazing and realistic painting of ducks on the water, Henry came walking up. He casually lifted his leg *and **peed** on the painting!*

Obviously we pretended we didn't know him.

And obviously the artist was *not* happy.

We moved on to another artist. His speciality was **ducks on umbrellas**.

While we were admiring them, Henry sauntered up to us again.

Then peed against this one too!

Whose warthog *IS* that?

Then we spotted
Ms. Woodhouse. She is an
incredible painter.

She specialises in
jump-splodge painting.

She'd painted a large flock
of ducks behind a splodge.

How *MAGNIFICENT is this
painting? Seriously.
It makes me want to weep.
And we know her!*

The second was of a small
family of ducks behind a
splodge. **Wonderful!**

One can *really* see how she
got to have what is
*probably the world's most
important art job* -
teaching at our school,
Swedhump Elementary.

And then her third one,
her *masterpiece*, was of
a single, lone duck,
admiring a **sunset**, but
behind a splash.

Amazing.

Henry sauntered up. This
time *even he* was
impressed.

How could anyone or anything
not be impresssed by this?
Admit it, you are too. And if you
aren't, well then **I feel sorry for**
you because you don't understand
anything about art!

Then we heard a scream.
Three screams to be more
specific. Wombattina-type
screams.

Uh oh! Was our peaceful
morning about to become
very un-peaceful?

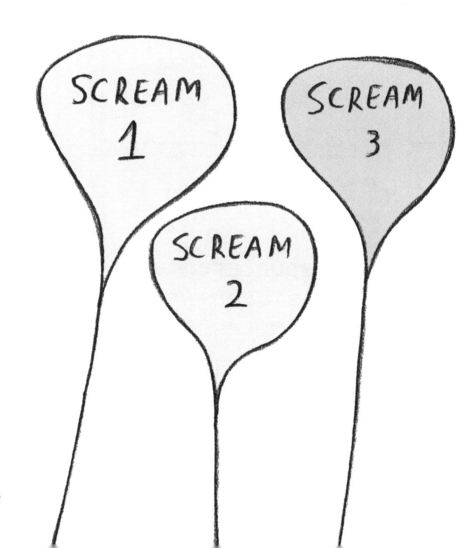

Chapter 4
The Trail

We sprinted
down to the
source of the
screams.

The Wombattina triplets
were at the edge of the
lake, **flapping** their arms
wildly and *squawking*.

Were they pretending to
be ducks?

Were they trying to take off *and fly?*

The ducks
have all
disappeared!

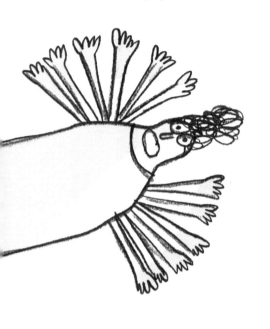

They've all
disappeared,
the ducks!

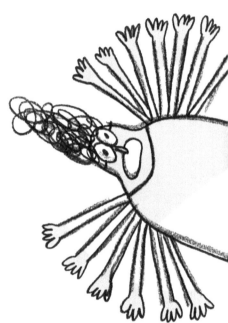

The disappeared,
they've all been
ducked!

And by gosh m'hock, they
were **right**.
There was *not a single*
Fluff-tailed Hemple-fluffer
to be seen **anywhere** on
Zoo Lake!

Look!
ZERO
ducks!

What the heggleswick was going on?

Rob pulled out his
<u>FM67</u>, one of the most
sophisticated duck-
finding devices on the
market.

Nothing.
Not a single beep.

Or quack.

But then a **small**, *very faint* **red dot** on the screen.

It had picked up something.

THERE!

It was indeed a
Fluff-tailed
Hemple-fluffer
disappearing **into the**
bullrushes at the far end
of the lake.

We ran over as
fast as we could.

The duck was just up
ahead, waddling fast and
furiously.

Then we saw why.

It was excitedly
gobbling up a trail
of bread crumbs.

The crumb trail wound
its way through the
bullrushes and then
into...

...a <u>snozzle</u>!

The duck disappeared
into it.

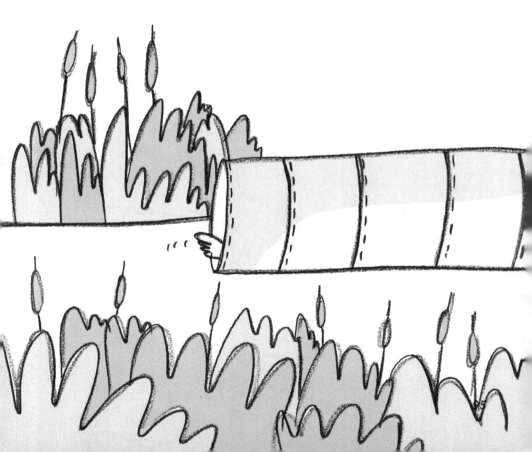

We followed the snozzle
as it wound through the
bullrushes...

...up a slope...

...and into a
wall!

And not just
any old wall.

It was the wall of
the *abandoned fort!*

What was going on here?

The abandoned fort had been empty for years, and it was **STRICTLY OUT OF BOUNDS**.

Why would someone be trying to lure the Zoo Lake ducks in there?

Rob and I didn't even need to say anything to each other, or even make eye contact.

Best friends know when it's time for action.

Rob deployed his <u>backpack ladder</u>, I strapped on my <u>KB-15</u>...

...and up we went.

From atop the wall we saw
a most unusual sight.

A courtyard with hundreds
of ducks milling about.

They were
the **missing**
*Fluff-tailed
Hemple-
fluffers*
of Zoo Lake!

The funny thing was,
the ducks seemed
quite cheerful.

And we could see why.

There were **trampolines** to
bounce on.

And **slides.**

And *bouncy seats.*

A theme-park
for ducks!?

Odder still,
there were strange
machines following
the ducks around.

They were sucking up any
loose feathers and putting
them in a series of troughs
at the far side of the
courtyard.

Lucky duckies! Playing
all day and not having to
tidy up afterwards!

Across the yard we
saw some sheds and an
office, machinery,
and **lots** of boxes.

Then we noticed the
letters **PP** were written
on *absolutely*
everything.

On the buildings and
boxes and machines.

What the *heggleswick* did
PP stand for?

Poultry Playground?

Chapter 4
Aa-tchoo

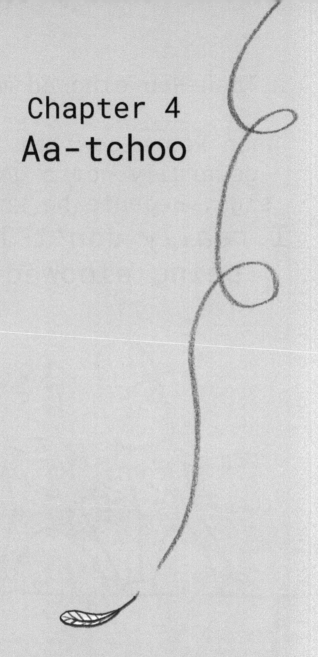

Then Rob elbowed me.

When Rob elbows me it's
generally not a good
sign. Because he knows
I *really* don't like
being elbowed.

He pointed to something further down, hanging from the wall.

It was a pod of scallywags!

And not just any old scallywags, they were **Feather-Scallywags**!

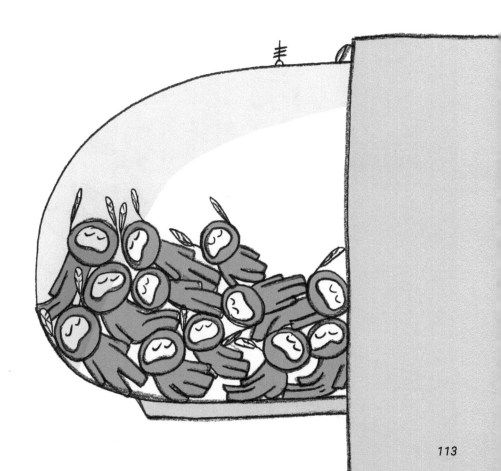

Why hadn't my KB-15
flashed!? Ah -
they were fast asleep.

**Lying-in on the
weekend!**

Luckily, Scallywags
aren't very dangerous
when they're asleep!

This KB-15 is
quite clearly
not flashing.

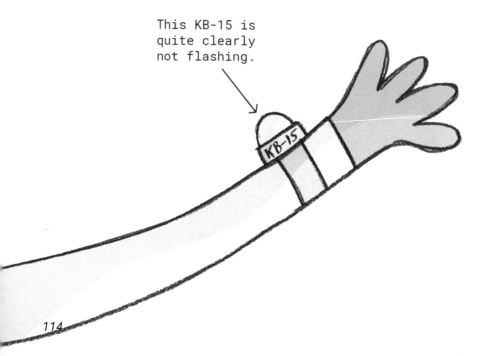

And I don't mean to scare
you but you should know,
when they're awake,
Feather-Scallywags are very,
very, very, very, very,
very, very, very, very,
very, very, very, very,
very, very, very, very, very,
very, very, very, very, very, very,

very, very, very, very,
very, very, very, very,
very, very, very, very, very, very, very,
very, very, very, very,

very, very, very, **very,**
very, **very,** very, very, very
dangerous.

We **definitely** didn't
want to wake those
scallywags.

I quietly took a <u>Neevil Eye</u> out of my backpack, attached it to the wall, *and started filming the courtyard.*

A Neevil Eye is a
RAD-SAW-CII
*(Remote Activated
Decoaguated Self-Actuated
Wireless Camera Interface
Interface)*, which lets
you spy on stuff safely.

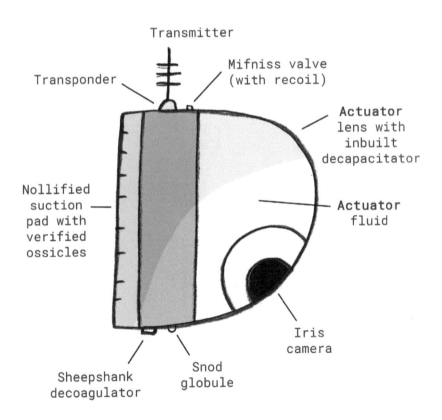

Transmitter

Transponder

Mifniss valve
(with recoil)

Actuator
lens with
inbuilt
decapacitator

Nollified
suction
pad with
verified
ossicles

Actuator
fluid

Iris
camera

Sheepshank
decoagulator

Snod
globule

Then Rob pulled out a
rope, attached his <u>G-hook</u>
to a groove in the wall,
and we silently shimmied
our way down to a pile of
cardboard boxes.

So far, so good.

We hid in the nearest box.

It was *very* comfortable.
Then Rob's nose **started**
twitching. Never a good sign.

Because, did I mention,
Rob has BAD allergies.
REALLY bad.

And we were hiding
in a box of *FEATHERS!*

Then Rob sneezed!

And when Rob sneezes,
boy does Rob sneeze.

This was **not good**.

Not good at all.

Sudenly my KB-15 started going crazy.

The scallywags must be waking up!

It was time to get out of there.

And fast!

But it was too late!

As we scrambled out, we heard an **ominous** *whirring sound* above us, a *small door* **shot open** on the wall, and a **net** fell *right on top of us!*

We were trapped!

Yet no scallywags
appeared...

...just one
nasty-looking man.

We had absolutely no idea
who he was, and clearly
he wasn't going to
introduce himself.

Let's call him
P-man, for obvious
reasons.

"Ah, our <u>MAWAWAWA</u>* seems
to work *very well!*"
he laughed.

*Movement-Activated Warning Alarm With
Autonomous Wobble Adjustment

Then his laugh turned
to a snarl.

"How dare you intruders
disturb my brunch!

Today I'm having **fry deggs**
on toast on bread on toast
on bread on toast."

"I'm going back to my eating parlor, but don't worry," he continued, laughing once again,

"there are some *lovely* Bograts here to keep you company!"

An eating parlor?

Bograts?

Who WAS this person *and what was he doing in this abandoned fort with all the Fluff-tailed Hemple-fluffers?*

And off he went.

We were well and
truly TRAPPED!

Then we heard a sound.

A scratching sort of
gnawing sound.

There was **something
scratching a hole in the
wall next to us**. Something
trying to *get* to us.

Please don't let it be a
Bograt!

Please!

It was the most terrifying
moment of my life.

Chapter 5
Two Total
Situations

Ok, where was I?

Oh yes....

AAAARRRRRRR-
RGHHHHHHHHHH!!
BBBBBBOGGGGGG-
GRAAAAAATTTSS!

And then we realized.

That familiar smell.

It wasn't a Bograt.
It wasn't a Grunt-leech.
It wasn't even a
Slug-mole.

*It was
Henry the Hog!*

Henry must have dug a hole
through the fort wall and
was chewing through the net.
He had come to rescue us!

T.H.S.

Total Hero Situation.

Chew Henry chew!

And FAST *because P-Man and the scallywags are near!*

After what seemed
like ages, I was out!

Just as I was untangling
Rob, my KB-15 started
flashing again.

*Something appeared
above us, and floated
down.*

A FEATHER!

And then another one, and
then another. We knew
what this meant.

And it was NOT GOOD.

Feather-Scallywags!

They had awoken!

"Atchoo!"
reezed Snob.

...I mean.
sneezed Rob.

And then I sneezed too.
And so did Henry.

A QUICK NOTE ON FEATHER-SCALLYWAGS

When they attack,
Feather-Scallywags release
a cloud of feathers.

This has
two effects
on the victim:

[1] Confusion   [2] Sneezing

Once you're sneezing, you simply
cannot fight (try it, you'll see
what I mean).

"Get them!"
bellowed P-Man.

This was serious.

The Feather-Scallywags
immediately deployed
encircle <u>Move 1,233
(Oxwagon)</u>.

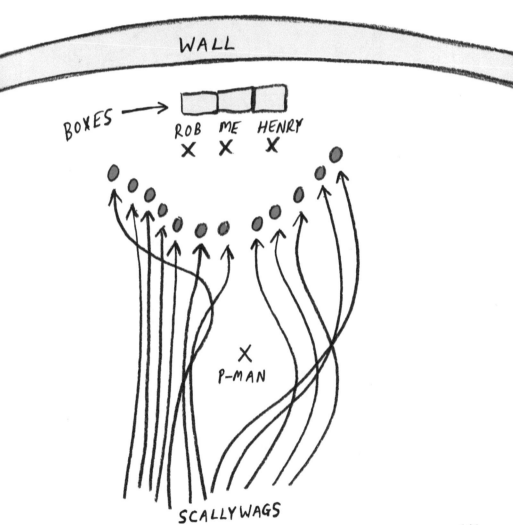

Then they **morphed** into their *signature attack* <u>Move 458</u> <u>(Feather-storm)</u>.

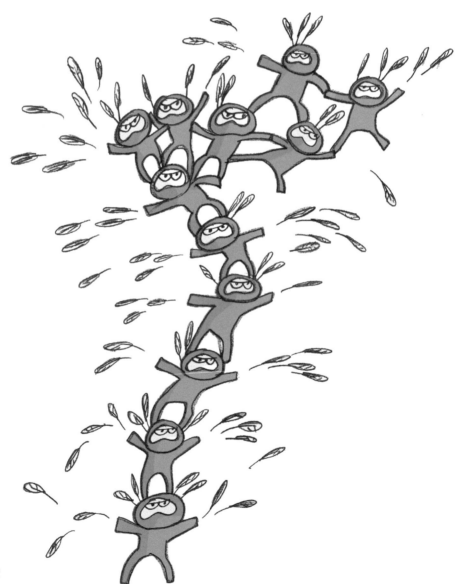

A wall of feathers bore down upon us.

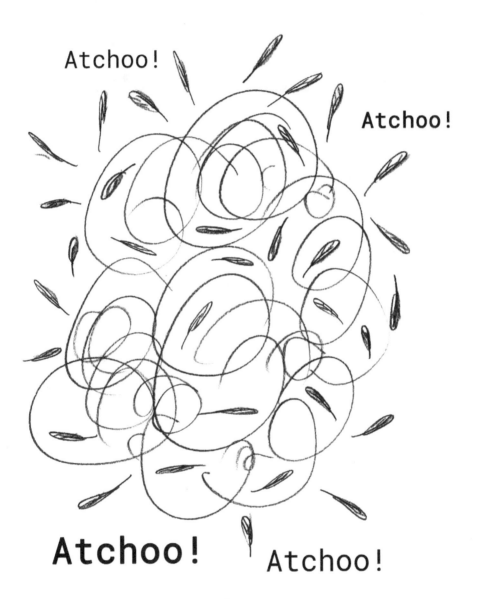

Atchoo!

Atchoo!

Atchoo!

Atchoo!

Atchoo!

But luck (and **Henry**) was (were) on our side.

Henry went solo with an *undocumented rogue move*, which Rob and I afterward christened **Ballistic-Warthog***.

*And successfully submitted the forms to have it included in the Almanac. It is now officially called Move 5,554 (Ballistic Warthog).

Sweeping the feathers aside
with his tusks, he gave the
most *terrifying* **bark-scream**
and went flailing at the
scallywags like some kind of
insane **inter-galactic
arachno-hog** going
completely berserk.

The scallywags hesitated
for a second - *a lull in
the feather storm* - so
Rob and I **took the gap!**

Instinctively we
initiated
<u>Move 887
(Spinning Cartwheel)</u>.

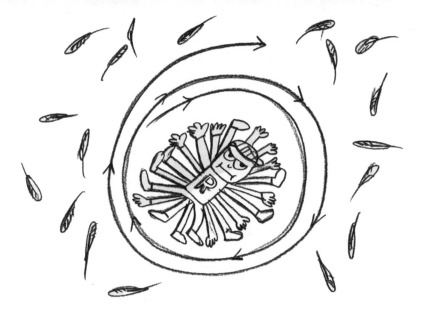

If done fast enough, the spinning creates a *fan effect* which keeps the feathers away.

It worked!

We cartwheeled towards
the snozzle.

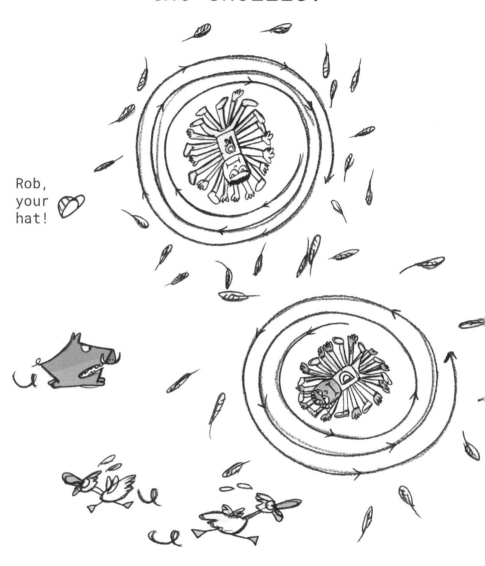

Rob,
your
hat!

Ducks scattered here,
there and everywhere.

Sorry duckies!

First Henry...

then Rob...

...then I escaped into
the snozzle. As I
entered, I removed a
RE (Rapid Expand) Ball
from my backpack.

It *immediately* sealed
the pipe behind me.

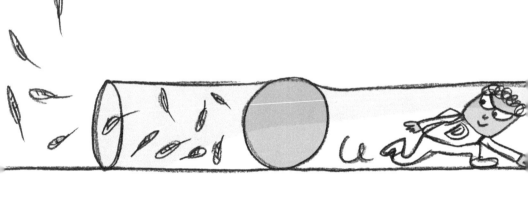

We were out!

Luckily Rob had a
replacement hat in
his backpack.

Well done Henry.

What a hero!

Chapter 6
The Chase

But then we
heard a
shout:

What!??

P-man and the scallywags
appeared atop the fort
wall and were staring
straight down at us!

We couldn't
believe *how fast*
they slid down!

They chased us *through* the bullrushes and *around* the lake.

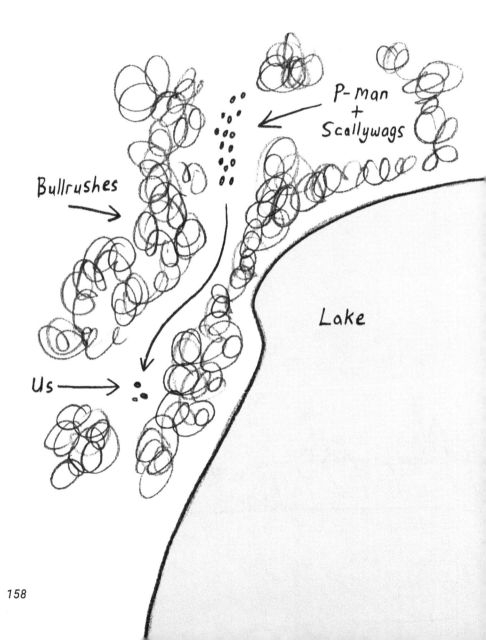

As Henry, Rob and I ran past
the Wombattina triplets
(still wet) they *glared
at us angrily.*

"So he's YOUR warthog!"
they shouted as we whizzed
past.

Then they saw P-man and the
scallywags on our tail.
The Wombattina triplets
joined the chase.

"GET THEM!" they all
shouted.

Then we ran past
Mr. Clanwilliam (still
wet) and the wedding
couple (even wetter).

It's that pesky
warthog again, and
he's with those
boys!

They joined P-man, the
scallywags and the
Wombatinnas.

"Stop them!"

And then, **oh no**, up ahead
was Cynthia Blappy and
her team. They'd just
untangled themselves.

It's that
dreadful
warthog!

Now the *entire* Tug-of-war
team began to chase us too.

Things were getting hairy.

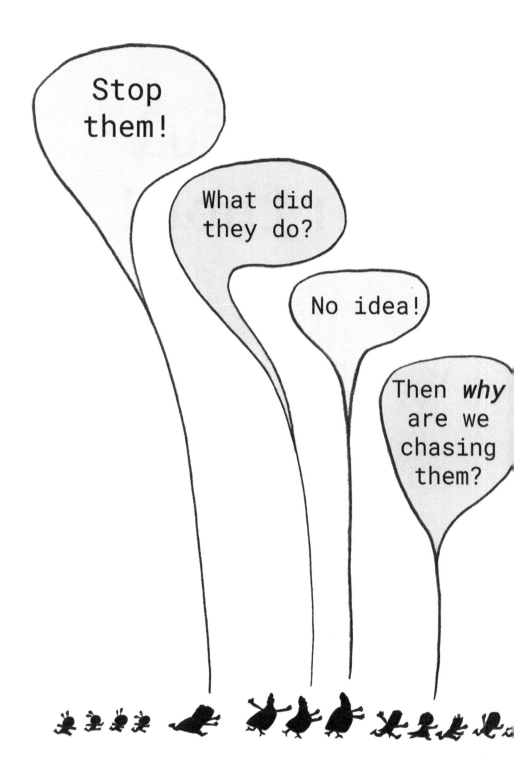

Time for *evasive action*.

As we sprinted across the grass...

I activated my
chameleon blanket...

...and *under it we dived*.

Poof!

Gone!

Our pursuers had no idea
where we were.

We'd simply vanished.

"Well!" said P-man
"IT'S PRETTY OBVIOUS THAT
THOSE HOOLIGANS AND THEIR
WARTHOG ARE THE ZOO LAKE
DUCK THIEVES, **OR MY
NAME'S NOT OCEANUS
POMINGTON!**"

*Better get out of
here quick before
they realize
what's up.*

"And now I'm going back
to my **eating** parlour to
finish my brunch!"

And with that he
was off, back to
the fort, with the
scallywags in tow.

If my deggs have
gone rubbery I'm
going to be
annoyed...

Chapter 7
Trapped Again

Oceanus Pomington?

THE
Oceanus
Pomington!?!!

I couldn't
believe my
earholes.

Have you heard of Oceanus Pomington? No? Well you'll **certainly** have heard of *Pomington Pillows™*.

NO?!!

It's only the *world's best* pillow factory. And do I need to tell you who the owner of the factory was....?

OCEANUS POMINGTON himself!

Pomington's Pillows™ are the best because they use only the feathers of <u>*Two-headed Fluffingtons*</u> which are the world's *second most fluffy ducks* - the fluffiest being Zoo Lake's Fluff-tailed Hemple-fluffers.

But one day Oceanus
Pomington **blew up** the
whole factory by mistake,
by over-cooking some
<u>umfalala pies</u>.

Everyone* knows how
dangerous umfalala
pies are!

Luckily he, his staff and the ducks mananged to get to the escape bunker **just in time**, and there were no major injuries.

But in the aftermath the ducks **ALL escaped**. And they've never been seen since.

And now *Pomington Pillows™* was **back**, with a **NEW** factory, and needing some **NEW FLUFFY DUCKS** to make their pillows the best again.

Lovely super-soft Fluff-tailed Hemple-fluffer pillows

Oceanus Pomington
was a no-good,
snolly-fogging,
hobble-gostering,
mumpfungus of a
duck thief!

Now stealing things is
not right.

You *don't* just go and
steal someone's tree
because you want a
treehouse.

You don't steal someone's **walrus** because you want a glass of <u>WOMBAT juice</u>.

And you **certainly** don't steal Zoo Lake *Fluff-tailed Hemple-fluffers* because you want to make pillows!

Ducks can be happy for a day or two in a play park, **but they are happiest when bobbing about on a lake**. Our lake. Zoo Lake!

Pomington needed to be stopped and **FAST**!

But convincing this crowd **wasn't going to be easy.**

I *can't believe* those boys are involved with the disappearance of the ducks!

182

This crowd was clearly
not on our side.

For the *time-being*, we
had **no choice** but to lay
there perfectly still and
hope they'd move off.

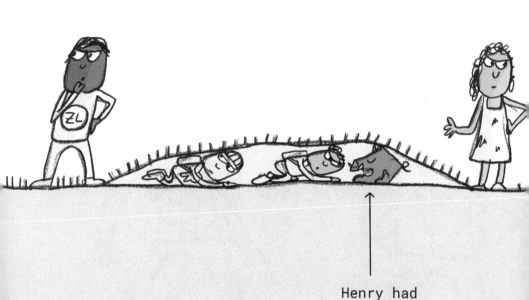

Henry had
meanwhile
started to
doze off.

But next thing something *very unfortunate* happened.

ATCHOO!

Rob sneezed!

Grass allergy!

Still asleep!

Our cover was **blown.**

Quite literally!

Now we were cornered.

Even Mr. Humma-Groff-Dwollop himself was there, and *not looking impressed* with us.

Chapter 8
Convincing a
Crowd

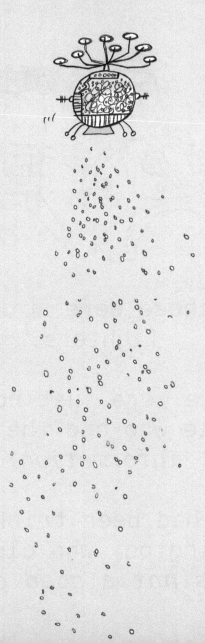

I guess we could have done **any number of things.**
(as you will have worked out, Rob and I are **VERY well equipped** to deal with *almost ANY situation.*)

But these were not enemy fighters.

These were just **normal** people who had the *wrong information.*

They had been **tricked** by Pomington, who clearly ***was not a good guy*.**

"Wait, wait, wait!"
I shouted.

"It's all a big misunder-
standing. We didn't *steal*
the ducks. We ***discovered***
the thief. And it was
Oceanus Pomington!

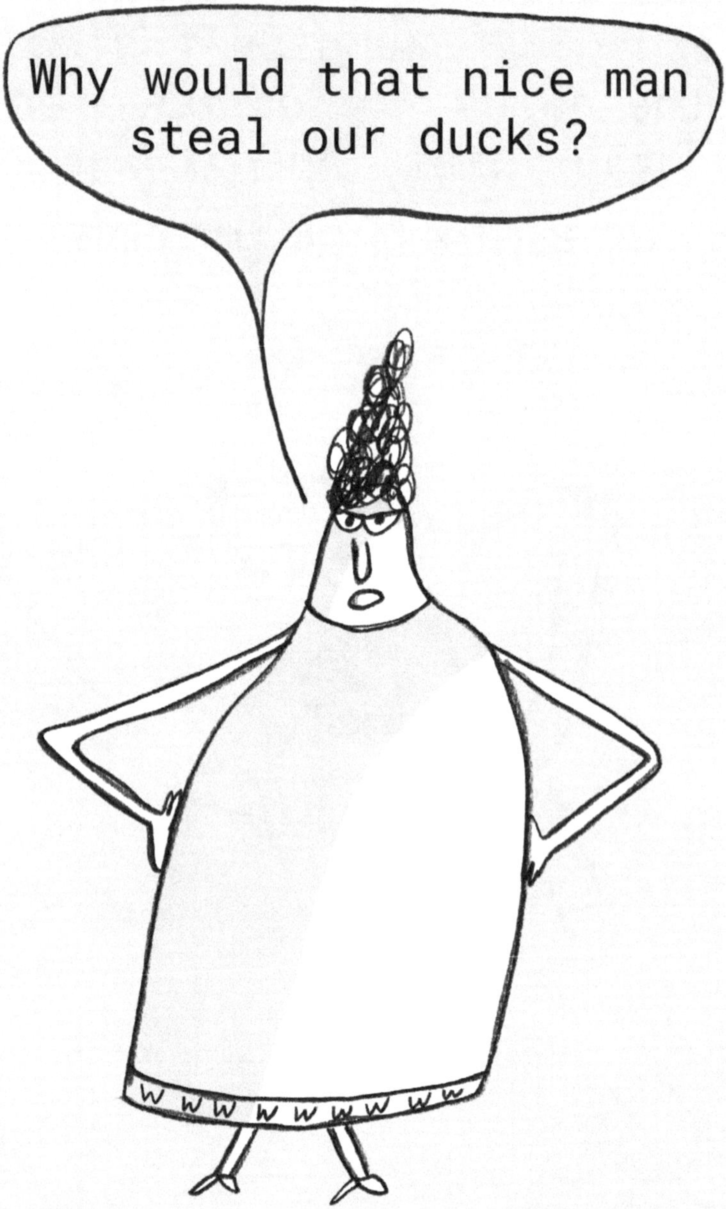
Why would that nice man steal our ducks?

"Do you have **ANY** *IDEA* who Oceanus Pomington is?"

No.

Um, nope.

No idea.

Nada.

"Oceanus Pomington is only *the world's MOST FAMOUS PILLOW-MAKER*, owner of Pomington's Pillows™, **that's who!**" 193

The crowd drew closer.

"Prove it!"

Easy!

I pulled an **EMP-767** _(Expandable-Micro-Projector-767)_ out of my backpack.

Rob pulled out a **SUFS44** _(Self-UnFolding Screen, 44 inch)_.

I then got the EMP-767 to
pick up the signal from
the Neevil-Eye I'd left
on the factory wall.

The images were
instantly beamed
onto Rob's
screen.

A yard *full* of
Fluff-tailed Hemple-fluffers
if ever I've seen one.

And there was
Pomington,
overseeing it
all.

I zoomed in so
everyone could
get a good look
at him.

Suddenly everyone started *crying*.

We miss our ducks!

Poor things!

This crew was cuckoo!

I had to find a way to keep them busy while Rob and I devised a **duck-rescue plan**...

Then I had a *JGI** if ever there was one.

JGI

*Jolly Good Idea

I quickly
deployed a **PMADD**
(Popcorn-Making-And-
Distributing Drone).

Everyone could watch
the ducks on the
SUFC44 while Rob and
I worked on the plan.

The PMADD showered
popcorn down.

Everyone
watched the
ducks
happily.

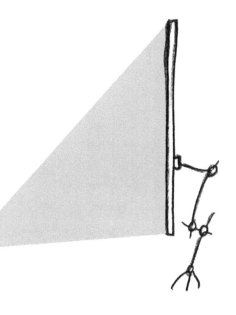

I pulled out my **QUIRIO** (_Quick-Release Instant Office_).

Rob, Henry the Hog and I huddled round and set to work.

Time for some brainpower!

Chapter 9
Plan 14p

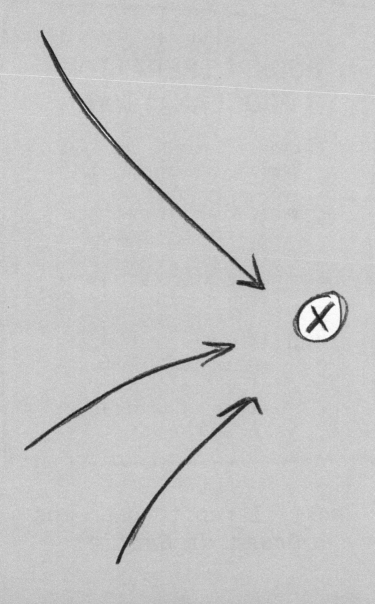

What we came up with,
which is now *very, very*
famous, was **Plan 14P**.

Using the EMP-767, we
projected it onto the screen.

Plan 14P
DUCK LIBERATION PROCLAMATION

Authors: Dash Candoo, Rob
Newman, Henry the Hog

Primary Aim: Liberation of
the Zoo Lake ducks

Secondary aim: Capture of
Oceanus Pomington

Tertiary aim: Defeat of
Feather-Scallywags

Weapons of choice:
Pillows

Next, I ran through the
Order of Battle:

ORDER OF BATTLE

[1] MAS (Mobile Attack Shields) deployed. DLS (Duck Liberation Squad) approaches fort gates.

[2] GHP (G-hook projectile) deployed.

[3] GHP attachment tightened and leveraged. Barrier perforated.

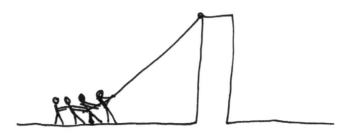

[4] MHU (Mobile Herding Unit) deployed.

[5] DSFA activated (Disciplined
Spear Formation Advance).

[6] AECA (Anticipated Enemy
Counter-Attack).

[7] DSARD (De-Shield and Rapid
Deploy). Enemy overcome.

[8] CU Alpha (Combat Unit Alpha)
engages Primary Target Oscar Papa.

[9] Conclusion of Battle.

We'd saved the *best* bit of the plan till **last** - how we would actually overcome the Feather-Scallywags...

Rob pulled a **PRD**
(Pillow Release Device)
out of his backpack. He
always carries one with
him, just in case.

He opened the lid,
and extracted a
pillow.

The fighters lined up,
and Rob distributed the
weapons.

SIDE-VIEW

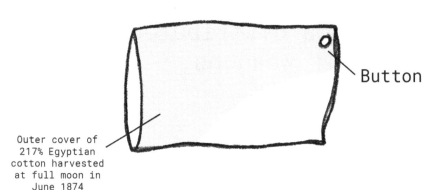

Button

Outer cover of
217% Egyptian
cotton harvested
at full moon in
June 1874

CROSS-SECTION

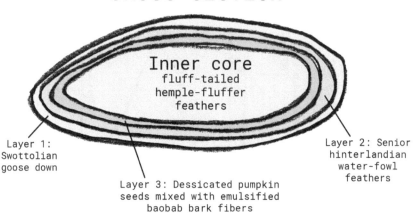

Inner core
fluff-tailed
hemple-fluffer
feathers

Layer 1:
Swottolian
goose down

Layer 2: Senior
hinterlandian
water-fowl
feathers

Layer 3: Dessicated pumpkin
seeds mixed with emulsified
baobab bark fibers

These weren't just any
old pillows, these were
JJ56s, stealth combat
pillows with inbuilt
invisible feather-shield
capability.

If the fighter squeezes the red dot on the corner, the shield automatically deploys over their head.

These pillows are also good for sleeping on.

ATTACK TEAMS

Boat 1
(spear head point):

Winnifred Wombattina
Winona Wombattina
Wilhelmina Wombattina

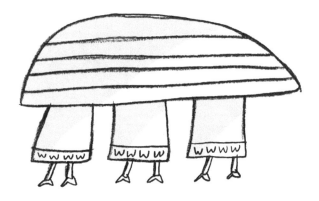

Boat 2
(spear head left):

Ms. Woodhouse
Mr. Humma-Groff-Dwollop
Mr. Darling

Boat 3
(spear head right):

Cynthia Blappy
Mr. Clanwilliam
Wedding couple

Boat 4
(spear shaft 1):

Tug-of-war
fighters

Boat 5
(spear shaft 2):

More Tug-of-war fighters

Boat 6
(spear shaft 3):

Artists

Boat 7
(*spear shaft 4*):

More artists

Spear Formation
by boat number

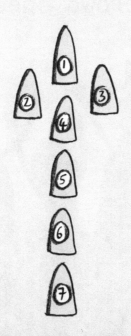

"What do you think?"
I asked.

The crowd cheered.

There was
no time to lose.

The Tug-of-war fighters
helped Mr. Clanwilliam
bring up the rowing
boats, and *we were ready
to roll.*

Our army approached
the factory gate.

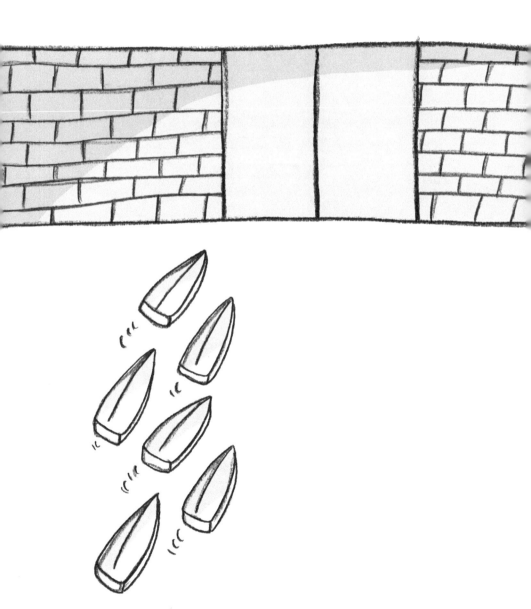

Things started off
calmly, almost as if in
slow-motion.

Rob threw the G-hook and
it caught.

Cynthia Blappy yelled **"Pull!"** and pull they did.

The gate *groaned* and held firm, but they **pulled harder**.

It opened slightly.
**Henry-the-Hog
took the gap.**

"**Pull!**" yelled Cynthia
Blappy, and **KRAKK**,
the hinge burst and
we were **IN!**

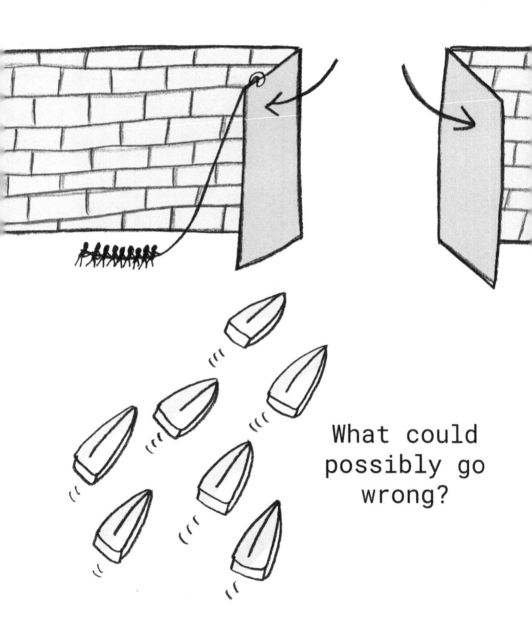

What could
possibly go
wrong?

Chapter 10
The Attack

The attack began.

Like a *precision swarm* of
disciplined *combat
cockroaches*, the boats
advanced silently in
PERFECT Spear Formation.

I was SO proud.

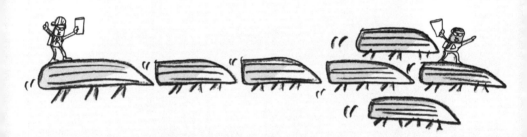

From atop the lead boat,
I shouted out the command
question:

From atop the rear boat,
Rob called the response.

Total Mayhem
quickly ensued.

A loud howl from Henry
and he started herding
the ducks as per Plan
14p. They began quacking
like crazy.

The noise woke the
scallywags and they
instantly **counter-attacked**
with a shower of feathers.

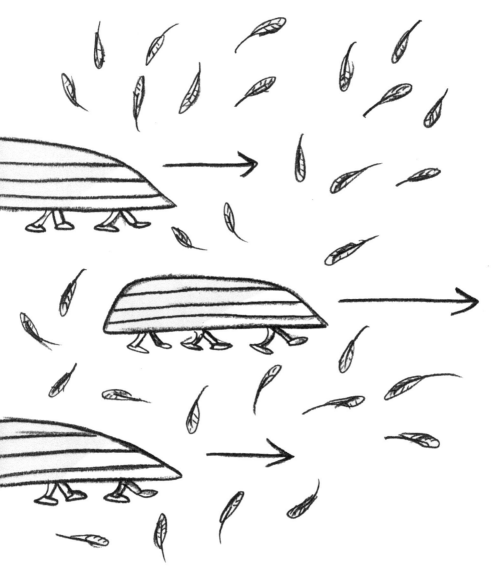

But the feather-resistant
upside-down boats kept
going.

The Spear Formation then fanned
out into a *perfect* Pincer
Formation, *just as planned*.

The scallywags now had multiple
targets to attack - and they had no
idea what these *huge wooden*
cockroach things were!

And the next thing,
totally terrifying for
the scallywags, the
stomachs of the boats
burst open and out came
the *screaming* fighters.

And because they were using
JJ56s, none of them were even
sneezing.

An **unbelievable*** battle ensued.

*Possibly the greatest pillow/feather fight ever fought. But unfortunately there was no official from the IPFA (International Pillow Fighting Association) there to witness it, or officially verify its brilliance.

But through the chaos
I saw we had a problem.

Henry's herding *was not going to plan*. The ducks were quacking and flapping all over the place *but not exiting* the fort.

Then the unthinkable
began to happen.

Scallywags **overwhelmed** a
few of our strongest
fighters.

First Rogina McRoger-
Rogerson (team captain
and Alpha-anchor)...

...**and then** Cynthia
Blappy *herself*!

And then
Mr. Humma-Groff-Dwollop!

This was the
penny-drop moment
for the ducks.

They recognised the man
who had fed them
baguette crumbs for *all
these years*, and
**they turned on the
scallywags in anger.**

TDAS!

Total Duck Attack Situation!

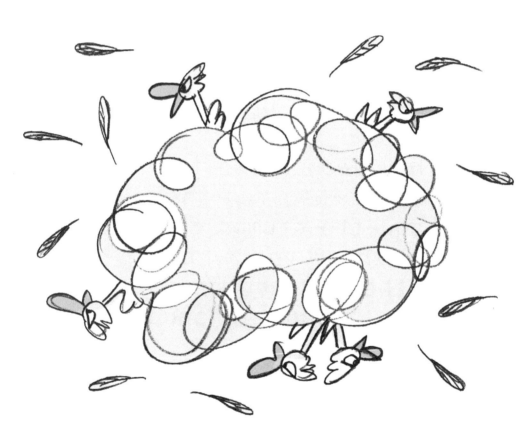

With the ducks now on
our side, we rallied
and counter-attacked
with such power that
the scallywags had no
idea what hit them.

They ran for their
lives.

Then we spotted
Pomington.

He had been hiding behind
a huge box of tissues*.

As he tried to sneak out
un-noticed, we pounced.

*Why a pillow factory needs tissues,
I have aboslutely no idea.

BANG!

Got him!

But Pomington was strong
and cunning and wriggled
free.

Oh no!

He was escaping!

Then, out of the blue,

TOTAL
HOGATTACK!

Can I just say, at this stage you might be thinking:

*Henry is quite small and Oceanus Pomington is a **fully-grown adult criminal**, so what's the big deal?*

But have you ever seen a flying warthog?

No you haven't.

A flying warthog is terrifying. COMPLETELY AND UTTERLY TERRIFYING.

Now where were we?

Oh, right,

TOTAL
HOGATTACK!

Henry

TOOK HIM DOWN,

and was followed by
three *extremely
aggressive* ducks that
were **thoroughly enjoying**
this whole combat vibe.

But Pomington was
super-slimy and slithered
free AGAIN!

And this time, *nothing*
was going to stop him.

Except some
baguettes!

HIGH-VELOCITY
SIMULTANEOUS
AIRBORNE
DOUBLE-LAUNCH!

Both *perfectly* on
target.

They hooked Pomington
around the legs and our
enemy *was down!*

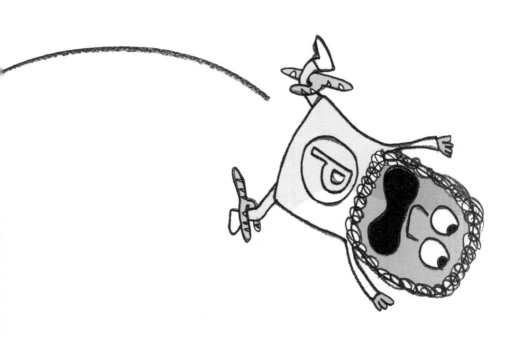

This time we were taking *no chances*. The triplets sat on him to make sure escape was NOT AN OPTION.

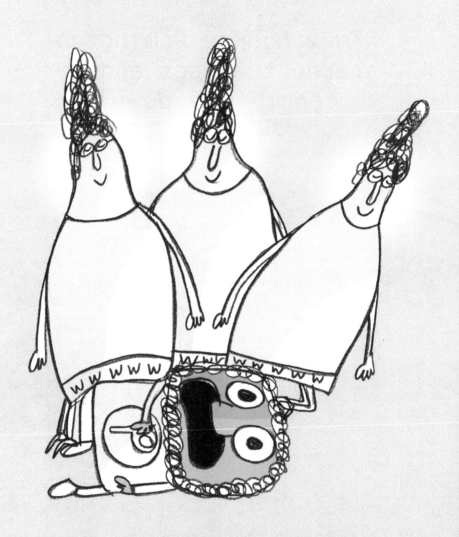

No wriggling free this time Oceanus!

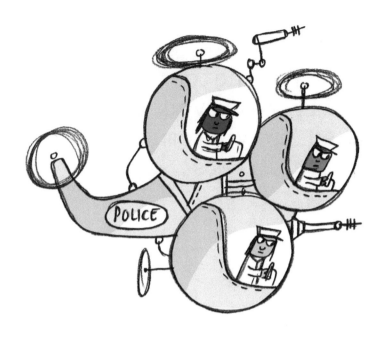

Rob used his SPIN radio
to call the police, and
within 37 seconds a
triplocopter had arrived.

Poor Pomington was
actually relieved to be
taken away from the
triplets.

They'd almost
squashed him
flat!

We watched as they
carried him away.

It wasn't **US** who'd be going for a *little holiday* on Witch Nose Island, **it was him!**

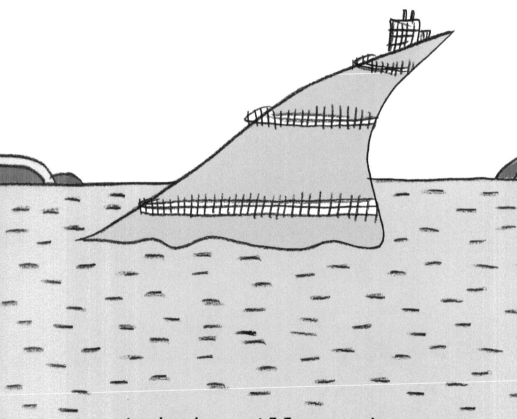

And the pillows there *aren't soft*, my friend. That much I can assure you.

Chapter 11
The Celebration

Back at the lake
there was much
cheerful laughter.

The ducks were all back.

To celebrate,
Mr. Humma-Groff-Dwollop
set his baguette machine*
to **Mode 88**, which as you
know churns out a fresh
new loaf *every 3 seconds*.

*A Lescure 89, the most
advanced and sophisticated
baguette-maker available.

The triplets did a *terrific*
triple dance for us.

The Tug-of-War team did a **weird** yet *brilliant* rope display, that included three ducks, two watermelons **and** a glass of <u>swamp juice</u>.

Clanwilliam showed
us his *fantabulous*
duck-balancing trick.

Henry-the-Hog did a <u>triplosault</u> around a projectile baguette.

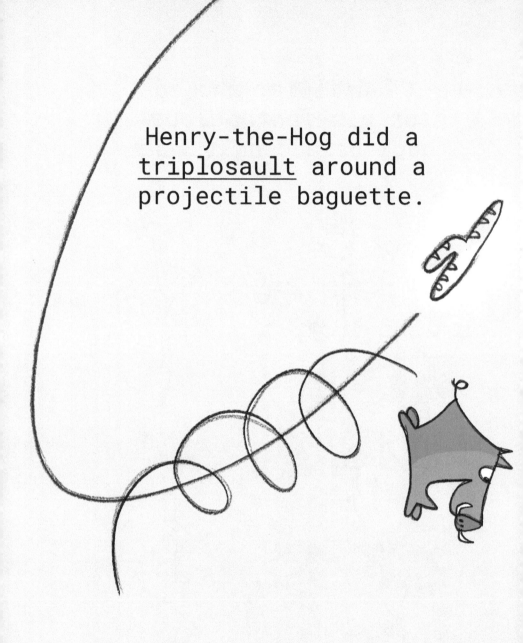

And Ms. Woodhouse
memorialized it all in a
most beautiful painting.

Told you Saturdays were good!

The end!

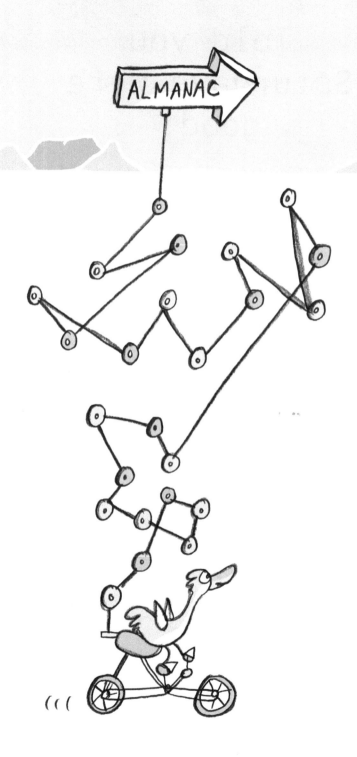

Almanac

The COMPLETE ALMANAC is the place where you can find out everything about Dash and his world.
It's online here: total-mayhem.com/almanac
What you're reading now is the Book 6 Almanac, providing detailed information for Dash Book 6 only.

Backpack-ladder

A backpack-ladder (BPL) is an important piece of equipment used by Dash and Rob on multiple missions. While very useful, it can also cause injury if incorrectly deployed. Accordingly, it is very important to have clean airspace over you when deploying. No low-lying trees or low ceilings, and obviously don't deploy inside an aeroplane, train, hovercraft or hot-air balloon. The same goes for reverse deployment. Make sure there are no obstacles above you. When carrying one of these, make sure the top of your backpack is correctly fastened.

In 2016, three employees at the BPL factory were injured during the testing process. The main backpack cover was not correctly fastened and the ladder expanded inside the backpack which then exploded. In 2019 a BPL auto-deployed in a factory staff member's car, causing him to drive off the road and into a shallow duckpond. Three ducks were injured and the factory had to pay a $25,000 fine. All three ducks recovered.

Bograt

A Bograt is a disgusting kind of rat that lives and breeds in only the vilest, smelliest bogs. They aren't actually dangerous, just disgusting. To have one come anywhere near you is an awful feeling, that makes even the bravest fighters shudder, shake, and sometimes start to weep. Luckily, these dreadful creatures are extremely rare. In fact, no photo has ever been taken of one, and no proper research has even been done on them, and come to think of it, nobody actually seems to know anything about them at all. Which makes us wonder whether they are perhaps made-up, and don't even exist?

Chameleon Blanket

Fantastic device that when deployed, instantaneously changes color to mimic its

*immediate surroundings, granting the user
immediate and effective camouflage. So if you're
in a desert and need to hide, just jump
under it. The blanket will look like the
surrounding sand. Highly effective in
fields and forests.
Invented by Mr. Rosebank.*

Deggs

*Deggs are eggs laid by Desert-quails.
They are like chicken eggs, but better.
They come in one hundred and thirty two flavors.
Their flavor is activated by what kind of mood
you're in, and happens automatically.
For example, if you're in a bad mood, the degg will
sense that, and become a flavor that cheers you up.
Main kinds are:*

Fry Degg   Scramble Degg   Poach Degg   Boil Degg

EMP-767 (Expandable-Micro-Projector-767)

*Highly compact yet very sophisticated projector.
Contains cutting-edge (and top-secret) technology
such as micro-snippet-processors, glandulated-
lens-rectifiers and emulsion proto-port-
oracles.*

*Manufactured by Savuti
Technologies Inc.*

Feather-Scallywags

*How common: Moderately
Special power: Feather-storms
Weakness: Sleepy
Typical group size: 12+
Operate alone? Never
Maximum Jump Distance: 7 feet
Cleverness: 6/10
Speed: 6/10
Agility: 7/10*

Fluff-tailed Hemple-fluffers

Extremely rare and very fluffy ducks. Especially their tails. The only place they are known to exist is on Zoo Lake. Highly sociable and live in one large flock as one family unit. Generally well-behaved and friendly, but when threatened can be aggressive. Their diet consists of grasses, aquatic plants, fish, insects, and their all-time favourite, Humma-Groff-Dwollop baguettes.

FM67

One of the most sophisticated Duck Finding Devices on the market. It is able to detect low-frequency quacks from distances of up to 5 miles. Manufactured by Rajak Industries.

G-hook

Invented by Greta Gretchen-Hoffer, this is a throwable hook that will catch on almost anything if thrown correctly. Super-light and super-strong. Made of krypto-web fiber. Dash, Rob and Greta always have them in their backpacks.

Gralarm

A gralarm is a Grisbium-type alarm. The one Dash uses is a Grisbium 800. This is a robotic alarm clock that will never fail to wake you up. While it is a machine, it is closely based on an actual real-life Grisbium. Grisbiums are creatures that live deep in The Foothills, and are noted for their sunrise anthems, officially known as The Grisbium Dawn Chorus.

Grozint Sandwich

Grozint sandwiches are delicious. Really delicious. By law they have to thirty ingredients or more. One of these has to be pickles. If they have no pickles, and/or too few ingredients, they cannot be classified as a Grozint by the GGCC (Global Grozint Certification Committee).

A food truck selling Grozint sandwiches once came to Swedhump Elementary and was very popular, but sadly just for a day. That's because on the second day, an inspector from GCIIA (the Grozint Central International Inspection Agency) arrived unannounced and analysed the sandwiches, finding only 28 ingredients. The owner was immediately arrested, and was only released after he paid the customary one hundred and forty eight million dollar fine.

Typical ingredients: Butter, pickles, degg , emfleffle, smushroom, snorringe rind, dried snail, banana peel, tomato skin, hummus, cheese, spinach, avocado skin, carrot, potato, peach, apricot, sardine, cauliflower, lettuce, baked beans, coriander, Swed eyelash, mustard, mayonnaise, ketchup, ketchdown, onion, chutney, boiled cabbage, grasshopper, oak bark, ant nectar, pumpkin root, pickled Osteop toenail.

Grunt-Leech
Grunt-leeches are leeches that grunt. And they suck your blood. They are disgusting. Here's a list of grunt sounds and their meanings, in case you encounter one:

Grünnt: Hello
Gruntt: Goodbye
Grrunt-grr-untt-untt: Where is the closest leech-hospital?
Gruüunt: Your blood tastes delicious
Grrrrunt: Your blood tastes awful
Ggggrrünttt: I have a headache, even though I don't really have a head
Grunnnnnnt: Can we be friends?
Grunt-grunttt-grünttttt: I wish I could ride a bicycle

SPECKLE DEGG IN REGULAR MODE

SPECKLE DEGG IN INVISIBILITY MODE

Invisibility Mode
This is when a person or animal or thing auto-invisible-izes, i.e. makes itself invisible. Devil-Cat knows how to do this very effectively. When Mr. Rosebank was young, he made a detailed study on

it but unfortunately the report somehow went into
Invisibility Mode itself. He searched high and low (and
medium) for it, unsuccessfully. This is what prompted him
to invent his now-famous Anti-Invisibity-Goggles. But it
was too late. The goggles took a year to develop and the
report was never found. It is believed the school cleaning
crew threw it into the trash by mistake. So sadly we can't
tell you anything about how Invisibility Mode actually
works. Sorry!

JJ56
Stealth combat pillow with inbuilt invisible feather-shield
capability. Press the red dot on
the corner and the shield deploys
instantaneously. Each pillow is
made up of a soft core, and then
three outer layers. They are
extremely light AND durable, so
ideal for combat. Each JJ56 is
hand-crafted and takes a team of
seventy-two technicians one week
to make.

Jump-Splodge Painting
Highly sophisticated and respected art form.
Jump-splodge painting involves jumping off a
cupboard onto carefully placed paint tubes,
which then shoot the paint onto a canvas or wall.

Ms. Woodhouse is probably one of the world's most
respected jump-splodge painters.

KB-15
Imminent Danger Warning Device (IDWD)

KB-15 Flash Codes:

* Red — on-off 1 second intervals
continuous: Imminent Danger
* Red — on 2s, off 2s: Imminent lightning
storm
* Green — on 3s, off 1s: Pizzup delivery
almost here
* Blue — on 5s, off 5s: Battery needs
charging

Krypto-web
World's strongest rope, it's made from the
leaf-fibers of a hammaphore tree.
It's so strong that not even
a Saw-toothed Doublodile
can chew through it.

Lescure 89
The Lescure 89 is the best baguette-making device on the
market. And not only does it make regular baguettes, the
customisation option allows a layer of flexibility that its
competitors can only dream of.

Modes:
(1) Regular baguette
(2) Fork
(3) Boomerang
(4) Number four shape
(5) Snake
(6) Nose
(7) Infinity
(8) Number eight shape
(9) Right foot
(10) Pi
(11) Over-shoulder hook
(12) We have no idea
     what this is - you?
(13) Brain thing
(14) Round thing

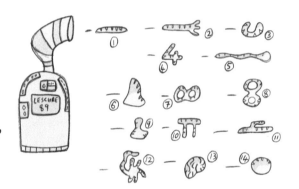

MAWAWAWA
The highly-sophisticated Movement Activated Warning Alarm
With Autonomous Wobble Adjustment can detect almost any
intruder, even an invisible one, and especially a sneezing one. Because they are very expensive, they are commonly
used to protect palaces, sensitive research centers, and the
homes/business/factories of master criminals. Manufactured
and distributed by Savuti Technologies Inc.

Move 458 (Feather-storm)
This is the signature move of Feather-Scallywags and it is
very, very, very dangerous. The scallywags form a tower,
which is usually quite top-heavy, i.e. more fighters at the
top than the bottom. They then spread their arms and begin

shooting out feathers.
The terrifying result is
an immediate, intense,
blinding feather-storm.
Enemies with any kind
of allergy are advised
to get out of there
immediately.

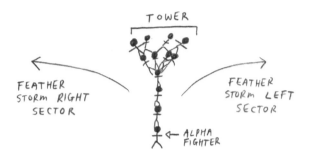

Move 887 (Spinning Cartwheel)

This complex and technical one is perfect for containing
and repelling Move 458 (Feather-storm). The fighter uses
a regular cartwheel with then morphs into a high-speed
spinning wheel.

Move 1,233 (Oxwagon)

Attack encircling move often used by Feather-Scallywags.
For it to be effective, at least twelve fighters are
required. Often comes as a precursor to Move 458
(Feather-storm), which is the signature attack move of
Feather-Scallywags. If Move 1,233 (Oxwagon) is deployed you
need to [1] get out of there immediately, or [2] put on a
anti-sneeze device, or [3] respond immediately with a
robust counter-move (like 887 (Spinning Cartwheel)).

① CLUSTER	② FANNING-OUT	③ ADVANCE
POD →	RIGHT FLANK · VORTEX ZONE · LEFT FLANK	
TARGET	T	T

Move 5,554 (Ballistic Warthog)
This is a flailing, bark-scream move invented by Henry-the-Hog. Not restricted to warthogs - anyone can deploy it. Because it is a new invention, and did not originate in the actual Scallywag Academy it was quite complicated to get it included in the Almanac. Over two hundred forms needed to be submitted by Dash and Rob before the ANEC (Almanac New Entry Committee) accepted it.

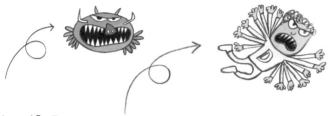

Neevil Eye
RAD-SAW-CII (Remote Activated Decoaguated Self-Actuated Wireless Camera Interface Interface), which lets you spy on stuff safely. Usually wall-mounted, although mosquito and spider versions (pictured) are available. It is water-proof, fire-proof and bullet-proof. It is coated with a micro layer of Genshin-Violet that tastes totally, totally disgusting, so is unlikely to get eaten by anything.

MOSQUITO
VERSION

SPIDER
VERSION

Once activated, it is constantly filming and data is automatically beamed out to a 10 mile radius. A receiver is needed to download the data.

Manufactured by Savuti Technologies Inc.

Pinkfish
Like goldfish, but a different color. Pink actually. Very tame when happy, but when bored can be aggressive and bite like pirañas.
Need constant attention, i.e. have to be walked,

entertained, read to before bed etc... Some rich pinkfish actually have their own walk-bowls. (Walk-bowls are bowls that can walk, in case you were wondering.)

PMADD (a Popcorn-Making-And-Distributing Drone)
Airborne radio-controlled popcorn maker that can feed over 50 people in one flight. Range of up to 100km. Manufactured by G & J Tarrow Siblings Inc.

Smaller versions for personal use are also on the market, and can dispense a range of different treats. There is even a refrigerated ice-cream dispensing version (the ICMADD). The TMADD (toaster version) is expected to be available next year.

PRD (Pillow Release Device)
Highly technical and top-secret device that can store up to 200 JJ56 pillows. We are not in a position to disclose where they are manufactured and how many are in circulation. Rob Newman always carries one with him, just in case.

Quadcycles
Four-wheeled cycles that can fold up into a backpack and be deployed by mind-activation. The wheel configuration constantly adapts to the terrain, and is controlled by a very sophisticated sensor (or "brain") embedded in the saddle. A quadcycle looks easy to ride but it is actually quite difficult.

A three-week introductory course at the QTA (Quadcycle Training Academy) is highly recommended.

Quadcycle Maintenance:
Pretty much the same as a regular bicycle maintenance, apart from the sneggle-sprocket. Keep the drive-chain clean and well lubricated, make sure brake-fluid pressure is good, check all nuts and bolts before and after big missions, make sure the tires are in good condition, and finally, and most importantly, make sure the sneggle-sprocket is smooth and has enough lemon juice on it at all times. Make sure the lemon juice compression canister is fully primed to at least level 8, especially before big missions.

QUIRIO (Quick-Release Instant Office)

Multiple different versions. In deactivated mode it reduces to the size of a match-box. The basic version has nine settings, based on seating requirement. So for example, if you want an office for two people, simply set the dial to two before activation. This version comes with an overhead extendable ramp for a small warthog, dog or cat, inbuilt electric chargers, seat-warmers and sinitercom capability. Pictured here is the basic version on setting one.

RE Ball

The Rapidly-Expanding Ball is very useful for blocking holes.

Four examples:
[1] Blocking the path behind you when you're being followed down a tunnel
[2] Sealing a hole in a dam wall
[3] Blocking a hole in the side of your aircraft to stop decompression
[4] Sealing the hole in a triplocopter fuel sump.

Reticulated Basingstoke

Probably Dash's favourite weekend breakfast.
Basingstoke is a kind of purplish moss that grows under
rocks and is totally delicious and highly nutritious if
prepared correctly.

It has a four day preparation cycle.

Best harvested on a Wednesday. Once you have the moss at
home, soak it in fresh avocado vinegar overnight, and then
on the Thursday morning, place it in a Reticulator for
24 hours. (A Reticulator is a specialised device for retic-
ulating basingstoke. Nobody really knows what reticulating
is, so don't even ask.) On Friday morning, remove the
basingstoke and place it in a bowl in the fridge for 24
hours. On Saturday morning, it can be served hot or cold,
and is delicious if you add some anchovies, a dollop of
vanilla ice-cream, a pinch of salt, fourteen medium-sized
chilli flakes, a teaspoon of bicycle brake-fluid, and one
sheet of shredded homework.

Sweds also love basingstoke,
but eat it raw.

Scallywags

There are many different types of scallywag.
Each type has its own fighting techniques, strengths and
weaknesses.

Slug-Mole-Slug

This can be quite confusing so you'll need to concentrate.
We're talking about two different kinds of slugs here:
slugs and mole-slugs.

A slug = a regular slug
A mole-slug = a slug that looks and behaves like a mole

Then you also need to know what a slug-mole is.
A slug-mole = a mole that looks and behaves like a slug.

SLIME
↓

So a Slug-Mole-Slug is either a
Slug-Mole-**Slug**
or a
Slug-**Mole-Slug**

A Slug-Mole-Slug = a slug that looks a behaves like a
slug-mole, i.e. it's a slug that looks and behaves like a
mole (that looks and behaves like a slug).

A Slug-**Mole-Slug** = a mole-slug that looks and behaves like
a slug, i.e. it's a (a slug that looks and behaves like a
mole) that looks and behaves like a slug.

Easy.

One day, if you're lucky, we'll tell you about Slug-Mole-
Slug-Mole-Mole-Rats. Now that gets complicated!

 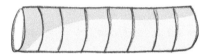

Snozzle
A snozzle is an expandable concertina-style pipe, i.e.
a pipe that can be retracted into itself to form a ring.
So it can be easily carried to a deploy location, and then
deployed, i.e. brought into effective action.

SPIN Radio
A SPIN Radio (Secure Police Interface Neo-
mogrifier) lets the user communicate directly
with International Police Headquarters. Very few
exist and only highly trained experts are allowed
to use them. It folds up to the size of a small
pea. Rob Newman usually has one with him.

SUFS-144 (Self-UnFolding Screen, 144 inch)
Fantastic device that can expand to the size of a large
cinema screen (30 feet high and 90 feet wide).
Manufactured by Rajak Industries. Because the SUFS-144
unfolds rapidly, users must be VERY careful when deploying
it indoors. In 2017, a technician from Rajak Industries
decided to take now home to show her husband. She deployed
it on setting 67 (maximum size) in their kitchen. The
screen opened so fast that it smashed right through the
ceiling and into the bathroom of the apartment above. The
upstairs resident, Walter Grumpleson, was having a bath at
the time. Luckily he wasn't hurt, but he was very annoyed,

and started yelling down at them though the
ceiling hole. It was not a very pleasant
affair. It took them 1 year to repair
the ceiling, and 3 years to repair
the relationship.

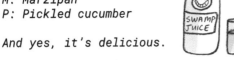

Swamp Juice

Swamp juice does not actually come from a swamp. Like many
of Dash's breakfast beverages, its name is an acronym:

S: Swed milk
W: Wombat juice
A: Artichoke juice
M: Marzipan
P: Pickled cucumber

And yes, it's delicious.

Swamp juice was invented by celebrity juice-ologost
Edwina Grottswenkle. She was actually on a beetroot
foraging expedition in the upper Foothills and got trapped
in her tent during a snowstorm. The ingredients of what we
now know as swamp juice are all that she had in her backpack. Luckily she had a mixer-mincer-shredder-liquidizer
in her kit, so blended them up for an hour (as per the
now-famous recipe). And luckily she also had a microwave
oven with her, which is what one needs to perfect the
process. She warmed it up to 225 degrees (as per the
now-famous recipe), then refroze it in the snow (as per
the now-famous recipe), then blended it again for 4 hours
(as per the now-famous recipe).

And voila, it was delicious. And a famous drink had been
invented!

Swedhump Elementary

Dash's school.
Principal: Mrs. Rosebank.
Probably the best school in the world.
Definitely has the best teachers in the world.
Named after the hump of a Swed, a two-faced humped creature.

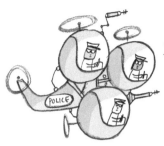

Triplocopter

Triple-helicopters invented by G. & J. Tarrow Siblings Inc. in 2010.
The equivalent of three helicopters stuck together. They are sixty one times faster and seventeen times more power-ful than regular helicopters, though more complicated to fly. The test pilot of the first version was James Hogsbottom, who teaches Paper Airplane class at Swedhump Elementary. There have been no reported triplocopter crashes to date.

Triplosaults

Triplosaults are triple somersaults.

A Grinning Triplosault is a triple somersault while grinning. A Grinning Jellybeanified Triplosault is a triple somersault whilst grinning whilst eating a jellybean.

The categorization goes as follows:

Somersault (single somersault)
Doublosault (double somersault)
Triplosault (triple somersault)
Quadrosault (4 somersaults)
Quintosault (5 somersaults)
Hexasault (6 somersaults)
Septasault (7 somersaults)
Octosault (8 somersaults)
Nonosault (9 somersaults)
Decosault (10 somersaults)
Nonononosault (99 somersaults)
Nononononononosault (999 somersaults)
Weirdosault (failed somersault)
Gronvosault (somersaulting into a wall — Gronville Honkersmith has been known to do this)
Plumbersault (when Mr. Plumtree does a somersault)
Summersault (a somersault in the summer)
Wintersault (a somersault in the winter)

Two-headed Fluffingtons

The world's second most fluffy ducks. The only flock
known to exist resided at the old Pomington
Pillow-Fighting factory before it exploded. The
ducks escaped unhurt but have never been seen
again. Some believe they are deep in Moremi
Forest. Other believe they live in the Foothills. Two-headed Fluffingtons can be very
indecisive creatures, and often the heads get
into arguments. It's actually quite a funny
thing to witness.

Umfalala Pies

Incredibly delicious pies made from umfalala fruit, i.e.
the fruit of an umfalala tree. Pick the fruits only when
they are completely ripe, otherwise they taste of wind-
shield-wiper fluid. Peel off the skin, slice them into

nose-shaped segments and then add them
to the pie-dough. Add lemon juice and
sugar. It is critically important that you
cut the pieces of fruit into the correct
nose-shaped shape. If you don't, the pie
will taste awful. Not like windshield-
wiper fluid, but like old soap. And old
soap tastes terrible. Much worse than new
soap, believe-you-me. One last thing.
NEVER over-cook an umfalala pie. They are
highly explosive when overcooked.

Vertical Tug-of-war

This is like regular Tug-of-war except its
vertical. The rope is thrown over a horizontal
beam. The aim is to lift the other team off
the ground. Each team consists of 5
pullers. The "alpha-anchor" is
the puller at the end of the
rope, usually the strongest
on the team. Olympic rules
declare that the horizontal
beam be exactly 18 feet high.

Warp-vortex

A warp-vortex allows the warpee (owner) plus sub-warpees
(passenger) to move from one place to another in a trilli-
second. Warp-vortexes are typically backpack-mounted.
Pocket versions do exist but are quite expensive.

Each warp-vortex has its own password, which the users will not share under any circumstances (so don't even ask).

Witch Nose Island

WItch Nose Island is the most secure prison ever. The entire perimeter is ringed by 27 krypto-web fences, 11 of which are electrified. The water around it is freezing and full of Shnarks (which are more vicious than sharks), flesh-eating, Saw-toothed Doublodiles and killer electric rays.
No prisoner has ever escaped from it.

Wombat juice

Wombat juice actually has nothing to do with wombats.

The name comes from its ingredients:
***W**alrus milk*
***O**ctopus saliva*
***M**ango*
***B**eetroot*
***A**vocado*
***T**omato*

Blend them in any proportions then serve with ice. Delicious!

Something is amiss at the Botanical Gardens.
Does it have anything to do with the mysterious helicopter
landings on Norma Island? That place is STRICTLY OUT OF
BOUNDS, which is why Dash and friends need to get there
fast to investigate.

The hatch was open and penguins were POURING out. "STAY CALM!"
yelled the principal, Mrs. Rosebank. "GO BACK TO YOUR
CLASSROOMS!" Dash and friends do as they're told, but when
something happens to their new classmate Ellen Ellenbogen -
linked to the world famous Ellenbogen Snausage Factory - 285
it's time to act, and sneriously fast.

The world's FUNNIEST and also MOST USEFUL joke book EVER.

743 laugh-out-loud jokes and then a HUGE INDEX at the back so you can find a joke for any occasion.

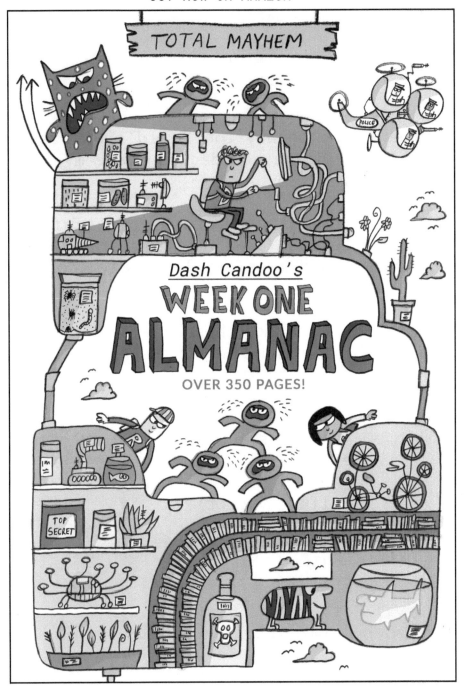

A MUST for any Total Mayhem fans, this Almanac is an
INDISPENSABLE accompaniment to the books, adding TONS of new
info to Dash Candoo's fantastic world.

Alphabetically-ordered for easy reference.

Dear reader-person,

Since I am probably the *World's Greatest Criminal*, I have decided to share my stories with you.

Please note that they are **DIFFERENT** *from the Dash Candoo Total Mayhem stories*. They are faster and messier, less text and **more like a comic**.

I've done them like this because I have *A LOT of them* and I'm excited about getting them into the world.

Follow my HILARIOUS ADVENTURES and mischief-making as I battle my arch-enemy, Bunny-Face.

I hope you like my stories!

- Devil Cat
  (Master Criminal)

www.itsdevilcat.com

Do you want to know why Devil-Cat is *so scared of watermelons?*

The answer actually involves an exploding watermelon, but it's such a long story that it takes over 80 pages to explain!

You can read all about it in THE ADVENTURES OF DEVIL-CAT Volume 1, out now on Amazon.

Smiley-Cola is the most popular cola on the market. But when Devil-Cat and Bunny-Face start selling their OWN concoctions, strange things start happening all over town.

NEXT UP! (and many, many more...)

If you'd like to be first to know about
our latest releases, subscribe to updates at
www.itsdevilcat.com/mailinglist

A few of the 100+ ⭐⭐⭐⭐⭐ reviews on Amazon and Goodreads

Bookwagon
Ralph Lazar's new series is shaping up to be one of the funniest (and silliest) in recent memory.

Reviewed in the United States on 11 April, 2022
Lazar's illustrations are the perfect companion for the wild and wacky story. One of the best aspects of this book is that there is an accompanying on-line almanac.

Lelah

my 7-year-old loves this series
Reviewed in the United States on October 10, 2022
My seven year old stays up late to read each new entry in this series. He's a big fan. It's a very approachable series if you are just starting out reading chapter books.

Kimberly J.

So Happy!
Reviewed in the United States on September 18, 2022
My daughter loves these books and reads them so fast and begs for the next one in the series. She hated reading before so this is a big step for her!

Susan M.

Silly, smart and a hit!
Reviewed in the United States on May 20, 2022
My almost 4 year old wanted this from the book catalogue, and I almost didn't get it for him because I thought it was too old, but I'm glad I did because we have read this book cover to cover three times in a week! He loves the story, which is just the right mix of silly and clever and the drawings. This is a GREAT book for a 4-6 year old to have read to them and also for an older kid to read to themselves. A must buy! We're back to get the whole series!

Go to www.total-mayhem.com for even more mayhem.

The only way we can continue self-publishing the continuing adventures of Dash and friends, is if we get lots of **reviews** (and ratings) on Amazon. This is because *the more reviews, the more people online get to see the books.*

So can we ask a BIG favour: If you liked this book, please can you write a review on Amazon (it can be just one line or even one word!), or at least give it a rating.

Thank you **SOOOOOOOO** much!!

Ralph & Lisa

Made in United States
Troutdale, OR
10/04/2023